Five Little Hearts

By Latrice Muldrow

Illustrated By Shey Kolee

Five Little Hearts

Published by Mission Publishers, Raleigh, NC
"Our Mission, Your Story"

www.missionpublishers.com
info@missionpublishers.com

Printed in the United States of America

Illustrator: Shey Kolee

ISBN: 978-1-7361050-6-1
Epub: 978-1-7361050-7-8

DEDICATION

This book is dedicated to my grandparents Anna and the beloved Joseph Muldrow, Sr., and the beloved Harry Sr. and Amy Adams. Each taught me that education is the key to a child's future.

Once upon a time,
Mother Heart and
five little hearts
lived on Rose Bush Lane.

Five little hearts
went out to play,
over the rose bushes
and far away.

Mother Heart said,
"Mi Amor, Mi Amor!"
Only four little hearts
came back.

Four little hearts
went out to play,
over the rose bushes
and far away.

Mother Heart said,
"Mi Amor, Mi Amor!"
Only three little
hearts came back.

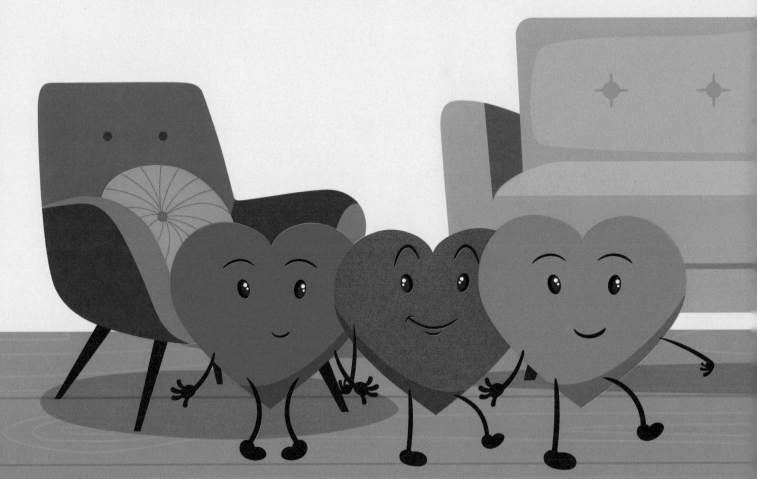

Three little hearts
went out to play,
over the rose bushes
and far away.

Mother Heart said,
"Mi Amor, Mi Amor!"
Only two little hearts
came back.

Two little hearts
went out to play,
over the rose bushes
and far away.

Mother Heart said,
"Mi Amor, Mi Amor!"
Only one little heart
came back.

One little heart
went out to play,
over the rose bushes
and far away.

Mother Heart said,
"Mi Amor, Mi Amor!"
No little hearts came back.

Poor Mother Heart was sad that day. She called, "Te quiero! Te quiero!" All the little hearts came back!

"THE END"

Glossary

Mi amor - My love
Te quiero - I love you

Five Little Hearts is both entertaining and educational. The story covers the adventures of Mother Heart, taking the five little hearts outside to play and using numbers to track their whereabouts. When the five hearts go from five to none, Mother Heart tearfully calls out to them, and they joyfully reappear playing in the yard. The book is heartwarming, fun, and a joy to read. It also introduces simple Spanish phrases.

Latrice A. Muldrow was born in Colleton, South Carolina and now resides in Raleigh, North Carolina, and has two sons. She holds a bachelor's degree in Family Consumer Science with a concentration in Child Development from North Carolina Central University and a master's degree in Child Development and Teaching Strategies from Liberty University. Latrice obtained her teaching licensure from birth to eight from the University of Mount Olive. Latrice has been an educator for over eighteen years and loves teaching students of diverse backgrounds.

Made in the USA
Columbia, SC
31 January 2025

53073982R00018